They needed to buy a birthday present for Max's daddy.

There was so much
to choose from.

What shall we get
Daddy, Max?

I know!

Dogs go Shopping

Sharon Rentta

Max and Mummy were going shopping.

Where did
I put my purse?
Did you see
Crufts last
night?
Do I really need a new
chewy stick?
SMALL
SIZES
AVAILABLE
PLEASE ASK

Max had some
brilliant ideas . . .

. . . but Mummy
said no.

Mummy wanted to buy Daddy **boring** presents.

PHARMACY
Do you want it gift-wrapped?
Yes, please.
SAY NO TO FLEAS!
Better?

"Can we look at
the toys?" said Max.

Hi!
They've got some really big sticks in the basement.
Oh, super!
sniff!

But Mummy was busy.
"Shall we get Daddy some perfume?" said Mummy.

"Careful . . ." said Mummy.

"Oh, Max!" said Mummy.
"I need you to be good while
I look at things for Daddy."

Max did **try** to be good . . .

but then he just had to go . . .

and find . . .

. . . the toys!
whee!
Can I play?

Wooo-hoooo!
Mine!
Mine!
All aboard!
Stop following me!

Now which toy would Daddy like best?
"I'd better play with them all,"
thought Max. So he played with…

an electric guitar

some roller skates

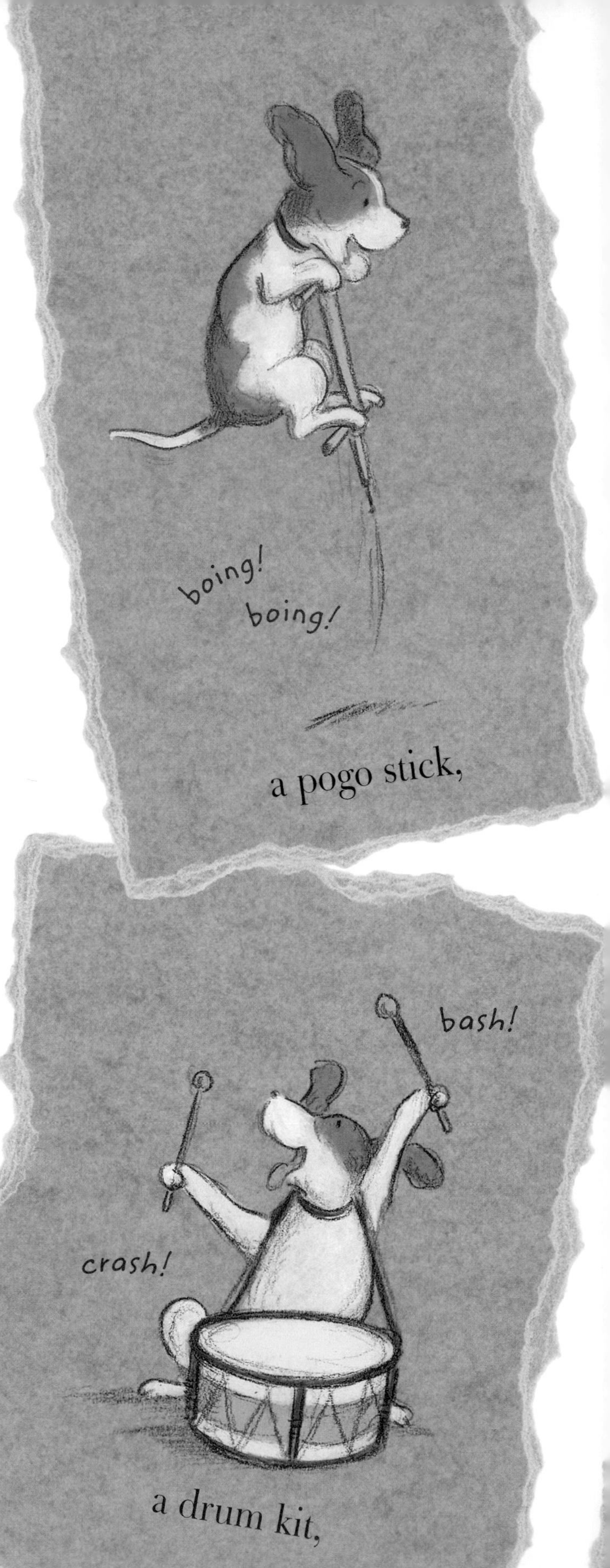

a pogo stick,

a drum kit,

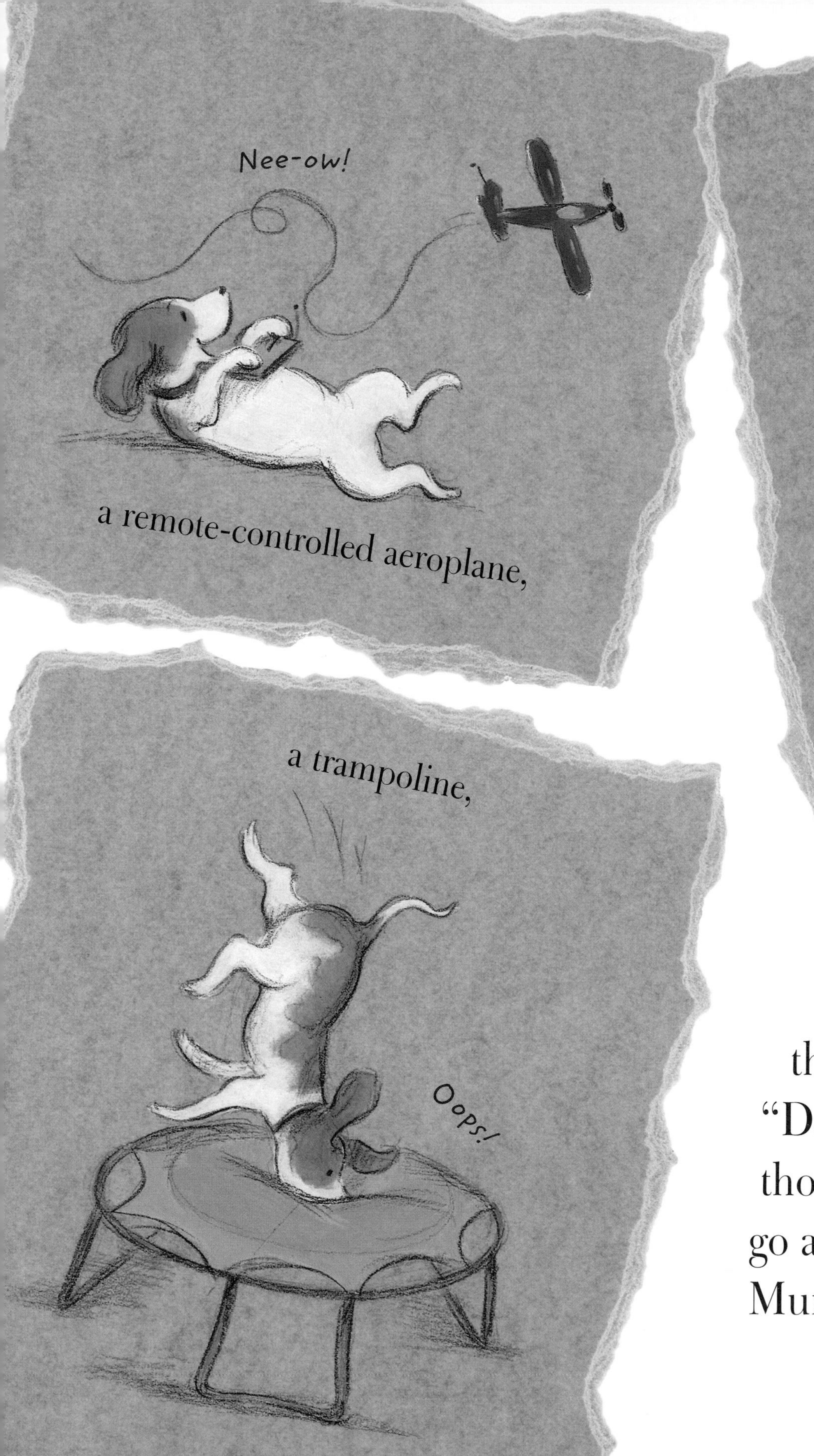

a remote-controlled aeroplane,

a trampoline,

Whee!

and a space hopper.

And then he found the best present **ever**. "Daddy will love this," thought Max. "I'll go and show Mummy."

But where was Mummy?
Max couldn't see her
anywhere . . .

Mummy?

Mummy couldn't see Max anywhere, either.

He wasn't in the Café.

He wasn't in the Bed Department.

He wasn't in the Opticians.

He wasn't in the Toy Department . . .

…or was he?

Max!
Woof!

"There's my puppy!" cried Mummy.
"Sorry, Mummy," said Max. "I had to find the toys, and then I found Daddy a skateboard and then you weren't there!"

Mummy couldn't be cross.
"I'm just happy I've found you," she said.
"Let's go and buy that skateboard."

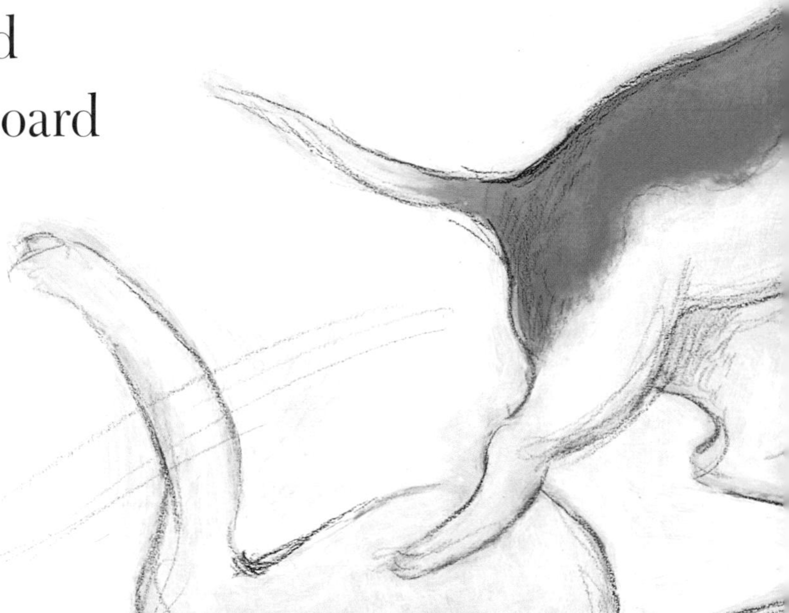

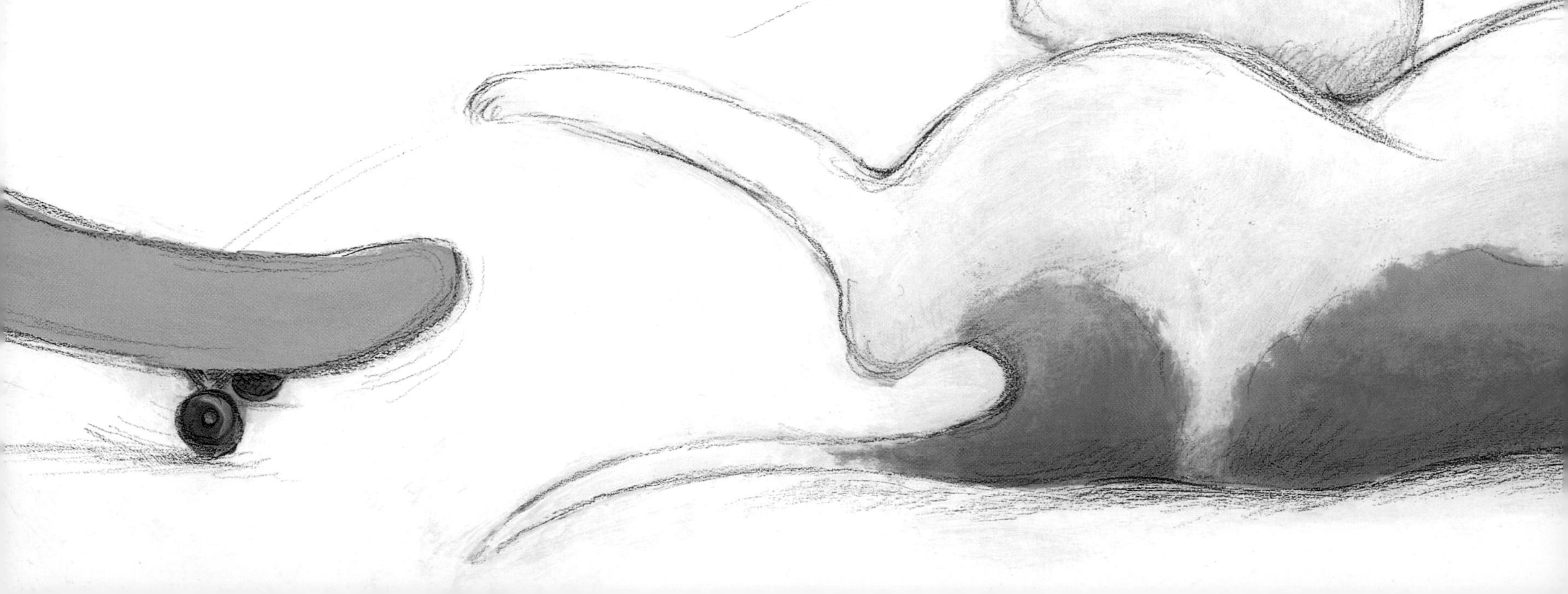

Aaah!
Mummy!
I thought I'd lost you!

Just for Dogs
No Cats, Please!
BARKER'S WALK
TOP DOG
Dogs' Diner

At last it was time to go home.
"Daddy's going to like my present best," said Max.

Go, Daddy!

And he did!

First published in 2010 by Alison Green Books
An imprint of Scholastic Children's Books
Euston House, 24 Eversholt Street
London NW1 1DB
A division of Scholastic Ltd
www.scholastic.co.uk
London ~ New York ~Toronto ~ Sydney ~ Auckland
Mexico City ~ New Delhi ~ Hong Kong

HB ISBN: 978 1 407108 61 2
PB ISBN: 978 1 407108 62 9

Printed in Singapore

9 8 7 6 5 4 3 2 1